Lost Love and Other Stories

JAN CAREW

Level 2

Series Editors: Andy Hopkins and Jocelyn Potter

Pearson Education Limited
Edinburgh Gate, Harlow,
Essex CM20 2JE, England
and Associated Companies throughout the world.

ISBN 0 582 42756 8

This edition first published 2000

NEW EDITION

Copyright © Penguin Books Ltd 2000
Illustrations by Peter Gibson
Cover design by Bender Richardson White

Typeset by Bender Richardson White
Set in 11/14pt Bembo
Printed and bound in Denmark by Norhaven A/S, Viborg

All rights reserved; no part of this publication may be reproduced, stored in a retrieval system, or transmitted in any form or by any means, electronic, mechanical, photocopying, recording or otherwise, without the prior written permission of the Publishers.

Published by Pearson Education Limited in association with
Penguin Books Ltd, both companies being subsidiaries of Pearson Plc

---

For a complete list of the titles available in the Penguin Readers series please write to your local Pearson Education office or to: Marketing Department, Penguin Longman Publishing, 5 Bentinck Street, London W1M 5RN.

Contents

	page
Introduction	v
Lost Love	1
The Doll	7
The Other Man	12
The Charm	16
Journey's End	20
Activities	25

Introduction

The house was dark and quiet.

But one hour later, there was a sudden noise in the night. Mr Brown sat up in bed. He was cold and afraid. 'What was that noise?' he wondered.

Mr Brown has a very quiet and sad life. But everything changes when he buys a doll. He hears voices. Things move and break. What is happening? Can he stop it?

The stories in this book are very different. They are all exciting and sometimes very strange. Some are sad and some are happy. But something strange happens in each story.

We meet many interesting people – a young man in love, a lonely customer in a shop, a writer at work away from home, a shy soldier, and an intelligent young man without a job.

Strange things happen to all these people. But life *is* strange sometimes.

Jan Carew, the writer of these stories, is also the writer of fifteen books for young people. She is a teacher, too, and now she teaches story-writing at Cardiff University, in Wales. She is very interested in other countries and other people. She visits different places when she can.

Lost Love

These things happened to me nearly ten years ago.

I lived in a city, but the city was hot in summer. I wanted to see the country. I wanted to walk in the woods and see green trees.

I had a little red car and I had a map, too. I drove all night out into the country.

I was happy in my car. We had a very good summer that year. The country was very pretty in the early morning. The sun was hot, and the sky was blue. I heard the birds in the trees.

And then my car stopped suddenly.

'What's wrong?' I thought. 'Oh dear, I haven't got any petrol. Now I'll have to walk. I'll have to find a town and buy some petrol. But where am I?'

I looked at the map. I wasn't near a town. I was lost in the country.

And then I saw the girl. She walked down the road, with flowers in her hand. She wore a long dress, and her hair was long, too. It was long and black, and it shone in the sun. She was very pretty. I wanted to speak to her, so I got out of the car.

'Hello,' I said. 'I'm lost. Where am I?'

She looked afraid, so I spoke quietly.

'I haven't got any petrol,' I said. 'Where can I find some?'

Her blue eyes looked at me, and she smiled.

'She's a very pretty girl!' I thought.

'I do not know,' she said. 'Come with me to the village. Perhaps we can help you.'

I went with her happily, and we walked a long way.

'There isn't a village on the map,' I thought. 'Perhaps it's a very small village.'

There *was* a village, and it was old and pretty. The houses were

black and white and very small. There were a lot of animals.

The girl stopped at a house and smiled at me.

'Come in, please,' she said.

I went in. The house was very clean, but it was strange, too. There was a fire and some food above it. I felt hungry then.

'That's strange,' I thought. 'They cook their food over a wood fire! Perhaps they have no money.'

I met her father and mother, and I liked them. They were nice people, but their clothes were strange.

'Sit down,' said the old man. 'Are you thirsty after your walk?'

He gave me a drink, and I said, 'Thank you.' But the drink was strange, too. It was dark brown and very strong.

I didn't understand. But I was happy there.

I asked about petrol, but the old man didn't understand.

'Petrol?' he asked. 'What is that?'

'This *is* strange,' I thought. Then I asked, 'Do you walk everywhere?'

The old man smiled. 'Oh, no, we use horses,' he said.

'Horses!' I thought. 'Horses are very slow. Why don't they have cars?'

But I didn't say that to the old man.

I felt happy there. I stayed all day, and I ate dinner with them that evening. Then the girl and I went out into the garden. The girl's name was Mary.

'This is nice,' she said. 'We like having visitors. We do not see many people here.'

We spoke happily. She was very beautiful. But after a time, she began to talk quietly, and her face was sad.

'Why are you sad?' I asked her.

'I cannot tell you,' she said. 'You are only a visitor here. We have to say goodbye tonight. You have to go now.'

I didn't understand. I loved her. I knew that. And I wanted to help her. Why did I have to go? But Mary said again in a sad voice, 'You have to go. It is dangerous here.'

So I said, 'I'll go to the next town and find some petrol. Then I'll come back.'

She didn't speak.

'I love you, Mary,' I said. 'And I'll come back to you. You won't stop me.'

She said goodbye to me at the door. Her face was very sad, and I was sad, too. I didn't want to go.

It was midnight. The night was very dark, but I walked and walked. I was very tired when I saw the lights of a town. I found some petrol, and then I asked the name of the village. But the man at the garage gave me a strange look.

'What village?' he asked.

I told him about the village. I told him about the old houses and the people with strange clothes.

Again he gave me a strange look. He thought, and then he said, 'There *was* a village there, but it isn't there now. There are stories about it – strange stories.'

'What do people say about it?' I asked.

He didn't want to tell me, but then he said, 'There was a big fire in the village. Everybody died. There aren't any people or houses there now.'

'How did it happen?' I asked. 'And why?'

'Oliver Cromwell killed them,' he said. 'He was angry with the villagers because they helped the king in the war.'

I couldn't speak.

'This isn't right,' I thought. 'That war happened 350 years ago!'

Then I remembered the strange clothes, the long hair, the food over the fire, and the old houses. And I remembered, too, about the horses.

'But I don't understand,' I cried. 'I saw the people and the village. I spoke to some people there!'

The man looked quickly at me, and then he spoke.

'There's an interesting story about the village. For one day every ten years, it lives again – but only for one day. Then it goes away again for another ten years. On that one day, you can find the village. But you have to leave before morning, or you will never leave.'

'Can this be right?' I thought. Perhaps it was. Mary said, 'You have to go.' She loved me, but she said, 'We have to say goodbye.' She was afraid for me. 'Now I understand,' I thought.

I went back to the village, but it wasn't there. I looked again and again, but I couldn't find it. I saw only flowers and trees. I heard only the sound of the birds and the wind. I was very sad. I sat down on the ground and cried.

I will never forget that day. I remember Mary, and I will always love her.

Now, I only have to wait two months. The village will come back again. On the right day, I will go back. I will find her again, my love with the long, black hair. And this time, I will not leave before morning. I will stay with her.

The Doll

Mr Brown lived near the centre of town, but his small house had a garden. Mr Brown liked his garden very much. It had a lot of flowers and they were pretty in summer – red, blue and yellow. Mr Brown liked sitting there in the evenings and at weekends.

But he had to work, too. Mr Brown worked in an office. It wasn't near his house, so he often went to work on the bus. He came home on the bus, too.

Mr Brown was a lonely man. He didn't have many friends, and he didn't talk to many people. And so he was sad and often bored.

One very hot day, Mr Brown walked home. He didn't want to go on the bus that day. He wanted a walk in the warm sun. In one street there was a small shop. Mr Brown looked in the window.

There were very old things in the window, and Mr Brown liked old things. He went into the shop.

'Good afternoon,' said the man in the shop.

'Good afternoon,' said Mr Brown. 'Can I look round the shop?'

'Please do.'

Mr Brown looked at the things in the shop. He saw an old doll with a sad face. It wasn't a pretty face, but Mr Brown liked it. The doll was a little old man with white hair and black clothes.

Mr Brown thought, 'Perhaps the doll is lonely, too.'

He asked, 'How much do you want for this old doll?'

The man thought. 'Oh, that. Three pounds,' he said.

Mr Brown wanted the doll. Why? He didn't know. But he wanted it. Three pounds was a lot of money for an old doll, but Mr Brown paid it. He went out with the doll in his hand.

He looked at its face. 'Is it smiling?' he wondered. 'No,' he thought. 'It's only a doll.' He said to it, 'I'm going to take you home.'

The doll didn't answer – it was only a doll. So why did Mr Brown speak to it? Because he was lonely. He put it in his case with his papers from the office.

Mr Brown was tired now, so he got on the bus. The man came for Mr Brown's money and Mr Brown bought a ticket.

Suddenly, somebody on the bus spoke. 'Go away!' said the person. 'You stupid man. Go away!'

Everybody on the bus looked at Mr Brown. 'Did he say that?' they wondered.

The ticket man was angry with Mr Brown. 'Why did he say that?' he wondered. He gave Mr Brown a ticket and went away. He didn't like Mr Brown.

When Mr Brown got home, he was very tired. 'Who spoke on the bus?' he wondered. He didn't know. He took the doll out of his case and looked at it.

It was only a doll. It wasn't very pretty. It was quite ugly but it had a smile on its face. 'That's strange,' thought Mr Brown. He put the doll on the table and had his dinner.

Mr Brown wasn't very hungry, so he only ate some bread and butter. Then he went to bed and slept. He forgot the doll. It was on the table.

Morning came, and the sun shone into the room. Mr Brown opened his eyes. There was something on his bed. 'What is it?' he wondered.

He looked, and he saw the doll. 'But I left it on the table. It can't walk – it's only a doll.' Mr Brown didn't understand it. It was very strange.

Mr Brown went to the front door. 'Are there any letters for me?' he wondered.

Yes, there were three with his name and address. But what was this? The letters were open! Who opened them? Mr Brown didn't know.

Mr Brown ate his breakfast. Then he went to the bus stop and waited. His bus came and stopped for him. Mr Brown got on with his case and sat down.

There were a lot of people on the bus, and one old woman couldn't sit down. Her face was tired, and Mr Brown was a kind man. He stood up for her, and she sat down.

Then suddenly, somebody spoke. 'You stupid old thing!'

The woman turned and looked at Mr Brown. She was very angry. Mr Brown's face went red. Then he remembered the doll.

He got off the bus. He couldn't understand it. 'That doll's at home,' he thought. 'Or is it?'

Mr Brown opened his case and looked inside. The doll was there, with a big smile on its ugly face!

He put the doll down on the street and left it there. Then he went to work. 'That's the end of that doll,' he thought. 'Good!'

Mr Brown worked well all day. After work, he walked to the

bus stop. But what was that? The doll was at the bus stop! Mr Brown saw the white hair and the black clothes, and he saw the smile, too. 'What's happening?' he wondered. 'It's waiting for me! It isn't only a doll. But what is it?'

He turned and ran away from the bus stop. Then he walked home. He had to walk three kilometres to his house. He was very tired.

Mr Brown sat down in a chair and went to sleep. He slept for an hour.

Suddenly, there was a big noise in another room – CRASH! SMASH! Mr Brown opened his eyes. 'What's wrong?' he wondered. He went into the other room.

The doll was there again. It sat on the table and looked at him. Mr Brown's cups and plates were all on the floor.

'It isn't only a doll,' Mr Brown thought. 'And it isn't a friend. This is difficult. What can I do?'

He took the doll into the garden and buried it in the ground.

'That really is the end of you,' said Mr Brown. 'You're under the ground now. You won't get out of there.'

Next day, Mr Brown went to work on the bus. He didn't have the doll now and nobody spoke. He worked hard, and he was happy.

Mr Brown came home again that night. He watched television. 'This is good,' he thought.

At eleven o'clock he went to bed. The house was dark and quiet.

But an hour later, there was a sudden noise in the night. Mr Brown sat up in bed. He was cold and afraid. 'What was that noise?' he wondered.

The noise was at the back door. Mr Brown was afraid, but he opened the door. It was the doll again!

It was dirty from the ground, but it looked at Mr Brown and smiled. It was a cold smile, and Mr Brown was very afraid.

He looked at the doll and said, 'Go away! Please! Go away!'

The doll didn't speak — it only smiled again. Mr Brown was very angry now. He took the doll into the garden again. He found some wood, and he made a big fire. He lit the fire. Then he put the doll on the top.

'Now die!' said Mr Brown. 'It's different this time. This *will* be the end of you.' And Mr Brown smiled. The fire was hot and red.

The fire got bigger — and bigger. Suddenly there was a loud cry, and people ran out of their houses. 'What's wrong?' they shouted.

'There's a big fire in Mr Brown's garden,' somebody said. 'Look!'

And there was a big fire.

The people looked round the house and garden. They couldn't find Mr Brown. But on the ground near the fire, there was a doll with white hair and black clothes. It wasn't a pretty doll. And there was a smile on its face.

The Other Man

I was a writer. I wrote books. I write now, but nobody knows. Nobody can see me now. Something strange has happened to me. I will tell you about it.

In January, I wanted to write a very long book. So I left my home and I found a little room.

'This is a good room for a writer,' I thought. 'I'll write my book here.'

It was a little room, but I liked it. It was very quiet. I began to work on my book and I was happy.

Then things began to happen – strange things.

One day I was at my desk with my pen in my hand. Suddenly, I thought, 'I want a coffee and I haven't got any. I'll have to go to the shop.'

I put my pen on the table and went out.

When I came back, I looked for the pen. It wasn't on the table. I looked on the floor, on my chair and then on the table again. It wasn't there!

'I don't understand it,' I thought.

That night another strange thing happened. I was in bed and the room was very quiet. Suddenly, I opened my eyes.

'What was that?' I wondered.

Then I heard a voice – a man's voice.

'Who's there?' I cried.

There was no answer and there was nobody in the room! I couldn't understand it, and I was afraid.

'What can I do?' I thought. 'What was that?'

After that, strange things happened every day. But I had to finish my book, so I stayed there.

The room was very small. There were not many things in it;

only a bed, a table and a chair. And there was a mirror on the wall. It was a very old mirror and I liked it. And then, one day, I looked in the mirror and – I saw him! The other man! It wasn't me. This man had a beard, but I didn't!

I shut my eyes and looked again. This time, I saw *my* face in the mirror.

'That didn't happen,' I thought. 'I was wrong. There wasn't another man.'

I went for a walk that day, and I didn't work on my book. I didn't want to be in the room. I didn't want to see or hear strange things.

At night, I went home again. The room was very quiet. I looked in the mirror and saw my face. But I wasn't happy. I went to bed, but I couldn't sleep.

'I'll leave here tomorrow,' I thought. And after that, I slept.

But then another strange thing happened. The other man stood by my bed and spoke to me.

'You will never leave here,' he said. 'You will stay with me.'

And then I opened my eyes. I was very cold and afraid. 'I'll leave now,' I thought. 'I can't stay here for one more minute.'

Quickly, I put my things in a case. I wanted to go – now. I couldn't forget the man, so I was afraid. But afraid of what? I didn't know.

When my clothes were in the case, I thought, 'I'll leave the room now.'

I looked round the room, and I also looked in the mirror again. And then I suddenly felt colder and more afraid. I couldn't see the other man in the mirror. Why? Because he wasn't there. But I couldn't see *my* face in the mirror! There was *no* face. Why not?

I tried to shout, but no sound came. I had no voice.

And then I saw him. I saw the other man – the man with the beard. But he wasn't in the mirror. He was at the table, with my pen in his hand. He wrote *my* book with *my* pen! I was angry and I tried to speak. But I couldn't, because I had no voice.

The other man didn't speak. He smiled and wrote.

Suddenly, there was a sound at the door, and I heard a friend's voice.

'Are you there?' my friend called. 'I want to see you.'

I was very happy then. 'My friend will help me,' I thought. But I couldn't move. The other man went to the door and opened it.

'Come in,' he said to my friend. 'Come and see my room. I'm writing my book.'

My friend came into the room, but he didn't see me. He smiled at the other man.

My friend said, 'Oh, you have a beard now!'

Again and again, I tried to speak but I couldn't. My friend couldn't see me; he couldn't hear me. He only saw the other man.

That is my story. The other man has my room. And he also has my face and my voice. He will finish my book, too.

But the other man doesn't know one thing. I can write – I can tell my story. And I'm telling it to you!

The Charm

'He's a brave man,' people say about me. 'He's never afraid.'

They are wrong. I wasn't always a brave man, and at times I was afraid – very afraid.

I am an important man now. I have an important job. People know me and like me. They don't know that I wasn't always brave. I will tell you the story.

I was a very shy young man. I didn't like talking to other young men; I was afraid. 'They'll laugh at me,' I thought.

Women were worse. I never spoke to them; I was always afraid of them.

I try to help shy people now. I never laugh at them, because I remember that time. I was very unhappy then.

Then there was a war between my country and another country. I had to be a soldier. Me! I was always afraid, but I had to be a soldier! And it was very dangerous.

I was afraid. The other soldiers didn't talk about it, but they knew. 'They're laughing at me,' I thought. '*They* aren't afraid.' I was wrong, but I didn't know that. I felt very bad.

One day, I was in the town. I had two days holiday, away from the other soldiers. I wasn't with friends; I didn't have any friends. I was very unhappy. I walked slowly past some shops.

An old man stood by the road. There weren't many cars on it.

'Why doesn't he walk across the road?' I thought. 'Is he afraid?'

I went near him, and then I saw his eyes. 'Oh,' I thought. 'Now I know. He can't see! He wants to go across, but he can't go without help.'

Other people walked quickly past him. They had to go to work, or to their homes. They didn't help him; they didn't have time.

But I had time – a lot of time. 'I'm not doing anything,' I thought. 'Why can't I help him? I won't be afraid of him.'

I took the old man's arm, and I helped him across the road.

'Thank you!' he said. His hand felt my coat. 'This is a soldier's coat,' he said. 'Are you a soldier?'

'Yes.'

Perhaps I said it in a sad voice. The old man put a hand in his jacket. He took something out and gave it to me.

'Take this,' he said. 'It will help you. Wear it, and you'll be all right. Nothing bad will happen to you.'

He walked away, and I looked at the thing in my hand. It was a small charm – pretty, but strange.

'It's a girl's thing,' I thought, and I put it in my coat.

The next day we went to war. I was afraid – very afraid – but I remembered the charm in my coat. 'Perhaps the charm will help me,' I thought, so I took it with me.

Suddenly I wasn't afraid. Why? I didn't know. Was it the charm?

It was bad that day. Men died all round me. 'Perhaps I'll die next,' I thought. But I wasn't afraid!

Our leader was a brave man. He was in front of us, and we followed him. Suddenly he was down. He fell to the ground and didn't move. The other soldiers stopped. They were afraid.

I thought, 'Perhaps our leader isn't dead. I'll go and see.'

I went to him. The fighting was worse now, but I wasn't afraid. 'I've got the charm with me,' I thought. 'I'll be all right.'

I brought our leader back to a better place, and then I looked at him. He was very white and ill, but he wasn't dead. His eyes opened, and he smiled at me.

He spoke – not easily, but I heard him. 'Go in front!' he said. 'The men will follow you.'

The men followed me, and we fought well that day.

After that, I was fine. Later, I was a leader too. The men were happy and followed me. People didn't laugh at me then.

'But is it right?' I thought. 'I'm not very brave. It's only the charm.'

I didn't tell people about the charm. I had friends for the first time, and I was happy.

One day we had to take an important bridge. There were a lot of soldiers on it, and they had big guns. The country was open, without any trees. It was very dangerous, and my men were afraid.

'We're going to die,' they said.

'Listen,' I told them. 'I'll go first, and we'll run very quickly to the bridge. Don't be afraid. They can't kill us all. Follow me, and we'll take that bridge.'

I put my hand in my coat. But the charm wasn't there!

'What am I going to do?' I thought. 'I can't be brave without the charm.'

I looked at the faces of my men. They weren't afraid now.

I thought, 'My words have helped them. They aren't afraid now. They're waiting for me. They'll follow me everywhere. I'm their leader, and I can't be afraid.'

I shouted: 'Let's go!'

We ran. We got to the bridge. We lost some men, but we got there! And we took the bridge!

I will never forget that day. I learnt something then about brave men. Brave men are afraid, too. But that doesn't stop them.

I will also remember that old man with the charm. 'It will help you,' he said.

He was right. I learnt to be brave without it.

I was a young man then, and now I am old.

I am a brave man, people think.

And, yes – they are right. I am.

Journey's End

Tom Smith was a nice young man. He wanted a job, but he couldn't find one. Many people wanted to work, and there weren't many jobs. Tom felt sad because he never had money for clothes or the cinema.

When he was younger, Tom wanted to be a footballer. He was good at football, and at tennis, too. He was good at every sport. But there were other, better players.

Now Tom had a new idea. He thought, 'Perhaps I can find a job in a sports shop. I'll be happy then and I'll have money.' But it was only an idea. It never happened.

He tried hard to find a job. He looked in the newspapers every day and he wrote letters for jobs – a lot of letters. But he never found a job.

One day he saw something in the newspaper about a fair in the park near his house.

'That will be interesting,' he thought. 'It's next Saturday. I think I'll go. Yes, I'll go. I'm not doing anything this weekend, and it won't cost much.'

On Saturday Tom walked to the park and bought a ticket for the fair. It was a warm summer day. The sky was blue, and the park was very pretty. There were a lot of flowers – blue, yellow and red. Tom felt happy when he saw them.

The fair was good, too. There were a lot of people there, and many different games. Tom played some games. He won a box of fruit and a book about sport. Then he bought an ice-cream because he was hot and thirsty.

'I'm having a good day!' he thought. He sat down and ate his ice-cream. 'Now, what shall I do next?'

Suddenly he saw, in large letters:

Tom Smith thought very hard. 'Shall I go in?' he thought. 'Why not? I'm not afraid of the future. Perhaps it will be interesting. Yes, I'll go in and have a conversation with Madame Zelda.'

So he went in. It was very dark inside. An old woman with grey hair and a kind face smiled at Tom.

MADAME ZELDA KNOWS THE FUTURE
....
Do you want to know about YOUR future? Come in and talk to Madame Zelda.

'Hello, young man!' she said. 'Sit down and I will tell you about your future.'

Tom sat down. The old woman looked at some cards on the table.

'Take three cards,' she said.

Tom took the cards and gave them to her. The woman looked at the cards for a long time. Then she spoke. She didn't smile now.

'Listen!' she said. 'I have to tell you something very important.

Do not go anywhere next Friday. Make a journey next Friday, and you will never arrive! Something will happen on the way. Don't forget now. I can tell you nothing more. Be careful, young man.'

Tom left. The sun was very hot on his face. He had no more money, and he wanted to go home. 'I'm not afraid,' he thought. 'I don't go on journeys. I won't go anywhere next Friday. Every day is the same to me. I haven't got a job, so I don't go anywhere.'

But on Thursday Tom had a letter. It was an answer to one of his letters! There was a job in a town thirty kilometres away. It was in a sports shop. The boss wanted to meet Tom the next day.

Tom felt very happy. 'I'll have to take a train there,' he thought. 'I can't walk thirty kilometres.'

Suddenly he remembered the old woman at the fair, and he felt afraid. 'Do not go anywhere next Friday,' she told him.

'But what can I do?' Tom thought sadly. 'I can't lose this job. It's too important to me. I'll have to take the train tomorrow. And what can an old woman know about the future? Nothing!'

But he wasn't very happy about it. And he didn't sleep well that night.

The next day was Friday, and Tom went to the station. He bought a ticket at the ticket office. The train arrived, and he climbed on it.

An old man sat down next to Tom. His face was intelligent under his white hair. He had a bad leg, and Tom felt sorry for him.

The train left the station and went through the country. A waiter came round with some food and the old man bought a sandwich. Then he smiled at Tom and said, 'Are you thirsty? I've got some tea with me. Would you like some?'

He took out a cup and gave Tom some tea. 'He's a kind man!' Tom thought. 'I really like him.'

He smiled at the old man and said, 'Thank you. I'm Tom

Smith. Are you going a long way?'

But the old man couldn't answer. Suddenly there was a very loud noise and the train stopped. What was wrong? The people on the train were afraid. They all looked out of the windows, but they couldn't see anything.

'Don't be afraid,' Tom told his new friend. 'I'll go and see. Perhaps it's an accident. Stay here and you'll be OK.'

The old man smiled. 'Thank you, my young friend,' he said. 'I will stay here. My old legs are very weak.'

Tom found the guard. 'What's wrong?' he asked him. 'Why did we stop?'

The guard looked at Tom unhappily. 'There's a large tree in front of the train,' he said. 'We'll have to move it, but we can't do it quickly. So this is the end of the journey for you. You'll have to get off the train and walk.'

'Walk where?' Tom asked.

The guard looked at a map. 'There's a village near here. You can go there and perhaps find a restaurant or a café. I have to stay here with the train. I'm very sorry about your journey. But you'll get your money back.'

Tom thought, 'The money isn't important. I really wanted that job!' And he felt very sad.

Tom didn't say anything about the job to the old man. He helped his friend off the train and carried his case to the village.

'Thank you very much,' the old man said to Tom. 'I know that my case is heavy. There's a computer in it, and there are a lot of papers.'

Tom smiled. 'It's all right,' he said. But inside he was very sad. 'I was stupid,' he thought. 'I didn't listen to the old woman, but she was right. I won't get that job now.'

The old man saw Tom's sad face and asked him, 'What's wrong, my young friend?'

So Tom told him the story about the job in the sports shop.

Then a strange thing happened. The old man smiled, and then he laughed! Why did he laugh? Tom didn't know and he felt a little angry. The old man was his friend, but this was a bad day for Tom. It wasn't funny!

Tom couldn't speak or smile. The old man saw this and he stopped laughing. Then he said, 'Listen to me, Tom, and don't be sad. I'm a rich man. I've got a lot of shops in different towns, and they're all sports shops. I want an intelligent young man to work in my new shop. It's also my biggest shop! Will you work for me? I think I know you now. You were very kind to me on the train. You're the right person for the job. What's your answer?'

'This is wonderful,' Tom said with a happy smile. 'This is the best day of my life, not the worst!'

ACTIVITIES

Lost Love and The Doll

Before you read
1 Answer the questions. Find the words in *italics* in your dictionary. They are all in the stories.
   a Ten years *ago*, what year was it?
   b Can you *bury* something in a garden?
   c What do people take to work in a *case*?
   d Can a *doll* think?
   e Has your country got a *king*?
   f When you are *lonely*, do you feel happy?
   g Do you get *lost* in your town?
   h Do cars use *petrol*?
   i Do you use your *voice* when you speak?
   j Do people die in *wars*?
   k When you *wonder* about something, do you know the answer?
2 What do you think?
   a Is *Lost Love* a sad story or a happy story?
   b In *The Doll*, why is a man afraid of a doll?

After you read
3 Work with another student. Have this conversation.
   Student A: You are the young man in *Lost Love*. You see Mary again. What do you want to do? Tell her.
   Student B: You are Mary. Listen to the young man. What do you think? Tell him.
4 What will the doll do next? Write some ideas. Then tell other students, and listen to them. Who has the best ideas?

The Other Man, The Charm and Journey's End

Before you read

5 Find these words in your dictionary.

beard   charm   fair   guard   leader   soldier   mirror

  a Which are words for people?
  b Which things do people:
     – look in every morning?
     – carry when they travel?
     – have on their face?
     – enjoy in a park?

6 Talk about your friends and family. Why are some people *shy*? Why are some people *brave*?

After you read

7 Strange things happen to the writer in *The Other Man*. What are they?
8 Discuss this question: What are these people afraid of?
  a the young soldier
  b Tom Smith

Writing

9 You are the young man in *Lost Love*. Write a letter to your parents. They will not see you again. Why not?
10 Write something for a newspaper about Mr Brown and the fire at the end of *The Doll*.
11 You are the writer in *The Other Man*. Write about a day in your life now.
12 The young men in *The Charm* and *Journey's End* are afraid of the future. Are they right? Are you afraid of the future? Why (not)?

Answers for the Activities in this book are published in our free resource packs for teachers, the Penguin Readers Factsheets, or available on a separate sheet. Please write to your local Pearson Education office or to: Marketing Department, Penguin Longman Publishing, 5 Bentinck Street, London W1M 5RN.